Teen Guide to HOBBIES

James Roland

ReferencePoint Press

San Diego, CA

For more information, contact:
ReferencePoint Press, Inc.
PO Box 27779
San Diego, CA 92198
www.ReferencePointPress.com

LIBRARY OF CONGRESS CATALOGING-IN-PUBLICATION DATA

Names: Roland, James, author.
Title: Teen guide to hobbies / by James Roland.
Description: San Diego, CA : ReferencePoint Press, Inc., 2025. | Includes bibliographical references and index.
Identifiers: LCCN 2023054424 (print) | LCCN 2023054425 (ebook) | ISBN 9781678208202 (library binding) | ISBN 9781678208219 (ebook)
Subjects: LCSH: Hobbies--Handbooks, manuals, etc. | Self-culture. | Mindfulness (Psychology) | Belonging (Social psychology)
Classification: LCC GV1201.5 .R65 2025 (print) | LCC GV1201.5 (ebook) | DDC 790.1/3--dc23/eng/20240124
LC record available at https://lccn.loc.gov/2023054424
LC ebook record available at https://lccn.loc.gov/2023054425

CONTENTS

How Hobbies Help

Skateboarding, playing guitar, baking bread, collecting autographs, building robots—just about anything can be a hobby. A hobby is something you enjoy doing on a regular basis that isn't harmful or unhealthy. Hobbies are fun ways to occupy the mind or body or both during downtimes. Though sometimes referred to as pastimes, hobbies are more than just a way to pass the time.

Alone or with Others

Hobbies can help relieve stress by taking your mind off school, work, or things that might be bothering you. Miquela Smith, who promotes gardening and plant education in the community through Texas A&M University, suggests that a hobby such as gardening has multiple mental health benefits. "Gardening is an excellent activity for practicing mindfulness, which is beneficial to overall well-being," she says. "The ability to use our hands, coupled with being outside, makes it less likely to be distracted by phones or other technology. This helps you focus and distract your mind from those things that would worry you."[1]

And when you can surround yourself with others who enjoy the same hobby, you suddenly have a sense of community. Friendships, based at first on shared interests, can grow beyond the ball field, dance studio, skate park, computer lab, or wherever you spend your leisure time with others. Alaura Prentice, a high school student in Tulsa, Oklahoma, took up dance at the urging of her father, who was part of a local Latin dance group. She says meeting others who also love to dance was one of the best things about starting her new pastime. "As a teenager, sometimes you feel that you don't belong in certain areas, and then you get to experience the hobby and you're, like, really good at something or you have a passion for it," she told *TulsaKids* magazine in 2023. "It makes you feel like, 'This is something I would like to do. This is where I belong.'"[2]

> **"As a teenager, sometimes you feel that you don't belong in certain areas, and then you get to experience the hobby and you're, like, really good at something or you have a passion for it."[2]**
>
> **—Alaura Prentice, Tulsa, Oklahoma, high school student and dancer**

Whether it's gardening, dancing, painting, cooking, or playing a musical instrument, hobbies can also help you learn new skills that you may use for the rest of your life. One other great thing about hobbies is that there is a nearly endless list of possibilities to choose from. If you're looking for something to do

Hobbies such as gardening can relieve stress by taking your mind off things that are bothering you. If you do them with others, they can also foster a sense of community and connection.

in the great outdoors, onstage, online, or in your room, you can find plenty of options. There are hobbies to do on your own, with a friend, with your family, or with people you've just met. "We often do leisure with people, and so it's a way to connect socially with others around things that we both like. And you wind up not just doing an activity, but sharing yourself, too,"[3] Matthew Zawadzki, an associate professor of health psychology at the University of California, Merced, told the *Los Angeles Times* in 2023.

Have Fun

Think about what you like to do or have always wanted to do or learn. Turning that into a hobby allows you to take that activity to the next level—improve your skills, learn more about something, or enjoy it in a new way. But keep in mind that whatever hobbies you pursue should be done for enjoyment. Perhaps the most important benefit of a hobby is that it's simply a way to have fun.

Don't think that your efforts need to be perfect or approach your hobby with the goal of impressing others. Hobbies should be diversions, temporary escapes from the demands of school or work. "If we put pressure on ourselves to be the best at our hobby, then we are equating it to our jobs, which is what we are supposed to get away from in the first place,"[4] says Selin Malkoc, a marketing professor at Ohio State University.

"If we put pressure on ourselves to be the best at our hobby, then we are equating it to our jobs, which is what we are supposed to get away from in the first place."[4]

—Selin Malkoc, marketing professor at Ohio State University

Mike Smith, a motivational speaker and founder of the nonprofit Skate for Change, a network of skateboarders who help the homeless in their communities, realized soon after he graduated from college that he didn't have to be the best at skateboarding, music, digital art, or any of his other hobbies to do something meaningful with them. "What I realized was those are industries I wanted to have an impact in," he said in a 2019 article on Medium. "My 'aha' moment was when I realized that if I focused my time on the impact I could have in those areas vs being 'the best' in those areas I could make something pretty special."[5]

You don't need to turn your hobby into a nonprofit organization, a career, or anything other than a way to enjoy yourself and maybe learn a few things along the way. Just remember that you can be as involved as you want to be with your hobby. It can be something you spend ten minutes a day doing or ten hours a week or more. And when you're ready to try something else, just know that you can always find a new hobby.

Hands-On Hobbies

What some people might call work, others call a hobby. At least that's the case for Greenwich, Connecticut, teenager Drew Hanna, who devotes much of his free time in high school to restoring and repairing old tractors. He even posts videos of his projects on YouTube and TikTok, earning him a devoted following and millions of views. "It's fun for me," he told the *Greenwich Time* newspaper in 2022. "What I love doing is figuring things out."[6]

Working with your hands to build, create, or fix something can be immensely satisfying and a lot of fun. And if tinkering with tractors isn't your first choice, you have plenty of other options. Just don't be intimidated if you've never picked up a wrench, knitting needle, or skillet. You don't need to be an expert; it should just be fun. In fact, some of the fun of hands-on hobbies is in learning new skills and mastering them as you go along.

If the idea of working with your hands appeals to you, look around at what friends or family members do or see how you can finally dive into a hobby that will keep your hands and mind busy.

Cooking

Your kitchen fills with the spicy scent of a fresh curry dish about to be served or the sweet aroma of cinnamon buns warming in the oven, and you are the one responsible for those mouthwatering delicacies. Learning to cook can mean much more than putting food on the table. Trying new recipes, foods, and flavors can be a way to explore other cultures, have fun with family and friends, and develop skills that you'll have for the rest of your life.

If you're a fan of cakes, cookies, and fresh bread, then you might like baking. And if you have an artistic side, you can take those baked treats to another level. Bradenton, Florida, teen Juliana Donnelly, who started cooking while her mother was recovering from a leg injury, makes cakes and cupcakes that satisfy her passions for baking and creative expression. "I love painting and drawing [and] all that, and sculpting. I do pottery," she said in a 2022 interview with Fox News in Tampa Bay, Florida. "You can do paintings [with] buttercream, you can do sculpting with fondant [icing], you can do, like, plating, all of that. There are so many options for design and, like, [the] sky's the limit."[7]

Baking treats is only one aspect of cooking; you might learn how to grill amazing steaks, stir-fry vegetable dishes, or serve savory soups. Whatever it is you want to make, you can find countless recipes online to keep you challenged. Going through

Cooking allows you to explore other cultures, have fun with family and friends, and develop useful life skills. It can also be a form of creative expression.

family cookbooks can also be a way to connect with parents, grandparents, and maybe generations who were here long before you. Some local restaurants even offer cooking classes, and some travel-abroad programs make regional cooking the focus of tours and hands-on lessons.

A 2023 survey conducted by the research firm Statista found that cooking and baking were the most popular hobbies in the United States, so you'll have plenty of company if you made a hobby of gourmet goodies, too. Cooking as a hobby is something you can start by simply using the pots, pans, and other items in your kitchen, as well as ingredients in your refrigerator or pantry. If a parent cooks a lot, ask to help with the next meal. Maybe the two of you can whip up some fun and create bonding experiences in the kitchen. Have friends over to cook together or to enjoy the dishes you make. Cooking is a hobby you can enjoy for the rest of your life.

Crafts

Putting your creative side together with activities that keep your hands busy can lead you to crafts that range from crocheting and knitting to making cards, calendars, scrapbooks, and much more. Little Rock, Arkansas, teenager Ananya Uddanti enjoyed arts and crafts when she was younger. She started looking for new creative outlets during the 2020 COVID-19 lockdown and decided to try making jewelry. She quickly found that she could turn anything from board game pieces to other odds and ends around the house into fun jewelry. She eventually began selling her creations online and donating the profits to charity. "It's clear to me that you can take something small at home, and just turn it into something a lot bigger than yourself,"[8] she told a local news program.

"It's clear to me that you can take something small at home, and just turn it into something a lot bigger than yourself."[8]

—Ananya Uddanti, teen jewelry maker

Choosing a Hobby

You may want to start a new hobby but not know where to begin or how to choose something that will keep you interested and entertained. Start by making a list of your interests. If you enjoy reading manga comics, maybe you'd also enjoy creating and drawing your own. Look at what your friends are into. Maybe you could join them in their hobbies or talk to them about how to get started. Spend time in hobby shops, arts-and-crafts stores, sporting goods stores, and other places while being on the lookout for a hobby idea that catches your eye. Also, be willing to try a variety of things. You may pursue half a dozen new hobbies in the years ahead. But before you spend a lot of money, see if you can start slowly, maybe with borrowed or inexpensive items, before you decide whether this is something you want to pursue with more energy and commitment.

To help you get started, stroll through your nearest craft store and see what looks interesting. Many larger craft stores, such as Michaels, offer in-store and online classes and workshops. And there's no shortage of bloggers and other online resources offering tips for beginners as well as more experienced crafters.

Model Rocketry

Kids have been building and shooting off model rockets since the 1950s, around the same time the United States and other countries began launching giant rockets into space. The sophistication of model rockets and the opportunities for rocketry hobbyists have skyrocketed since then. Model rocketry is a hobby that can fuel dreams of one day blasting off for Mars or inspire a career in aerospace engineering. It can also just be fun watching a rocket you put together blast off toward the clouds.

Most model rockets are powered by single-use engines that are a few inches long and can carry rockets a couple of hundred or, in some cases, a couple of thousand feet into the air.

You can buy model rocket kits at department stores, hobby shops, or online. You'll need a wide-open space like a school playground, park, or empty field where you can safely fire off your

Model rocketry combines technical building activities with the interactive fun of outdoor launch events.

rockets. You should also get the permission of the property owner or the proper authorities, such as your local parks department, before scheduling your launch.

Some communities have park space dedicated to local rocket clubs and rocketry enthusiasts. Joining such a club is a great way to meet others who share your interest and can help you get started. The National Association of Rocketry also has information about local clubs around the country. Your school might have a rocketry club, or you could help start one. And if you're especially ambitious, the American Rocketry Challenge holds annual competitions for middle and high school students to design, build, and launch model rockets. Teams are judged on the basis of their rockets reaching certain altitudes and speeds and landing with their payload—a fresh hen's egg—intact. In the spring

> "Once I learned about model rocketry, I wanted to share my interest."[9]
>
> —Vinay Vetticaden, high school model rocketry club founder

of 2023, a team from California's Canyon Crest Academy qualified for the national finals just two years after junior Vinay Vetticaden founded the school's Proxima Rocketry Club. "I got this idea because ever since I was a kid I thought that planes and rockets were cool," he told the *Del Mar Times*. "Once I learned about model rocketry, I wanted to share my interest."[9]

Gardening

What started as a 2020 COVID-19 lockdown distraction for Lattimore, North Carolina, teen Marlee Bivens and her mother, Holly Hicks, soon grew into a hobby that is benefiting others in their community. Bivens and her mom decided to have a contest to see who could grow the best cucumbers in their backyard. Bivens, who had never gardened before, won the contest. "I think I planted four of the seeds. I only expected maybe one to germinate and to grow. But all of them did, which was really, really rewarding,"[10] she told the *Shelby Star* in 2021. Before long, Bivens was visiting local nurseries and researching growing techniques. These days her room is filled with plants, potting soil, and other tools of her gardening hobby. She also established a community vegetable garden on land that once belonged to her great-grandfather to provide fresh food for those in the community who could use it.

Planting a seed and nurturing it into a lovely flower or delicious fruit or vegetable can be both fascinating and satisfying. Gardening can take on many forms, from a little plot of land in your backyard to some potted plants in your home or by your front door. Community gardens, even in large cities, also afford people the chance to dig in the dirt and help feed or beautify a neighborhood.

To make gardening a hobby, you just need a little soil, a few seeds, and the dedication to tend to your plants. Local nurseries and plant stores can be great sources of the supplies you'll need

The Origin of the Term *Hobby*

The word *hobby* got its origins in the fifteenth century, when it was used to describe a small horse, one that a child might ride or use to pull a little cart. Before long, the phrase "riding a hobbyhorse" was used to describe something that was frivolous or childlike. Over time, that phrase was shortened to the word *hobby*, but it meant the same thing. Collecting things and making things for any purpose other than selling them for money were seen as eccentric wastes of time. Aside from wealthy people who could indulge in pursuits such as painting or playing music for fun, nearly everyone else had no time or interest in what are considered hobbies today.

It wasn't until the 19th century that having a hobby became something that was socially acceptable and the mark of a well-rounded individual. Historians have also noted that many people in the United States took up hobbies during World War II to help distract them from the uncertainty and struggle of the war. Similarly, during the early months of the COVID-19 pandemic, people pursued new hobbies to help them get through those stressful days. Hobbies have indeed gone from activities once viewed as unimportant to helpful distractions to get through difficult times.

to get started and the advice that will help you avoid problems down the road. Many communities also have gardening clubs made up of volunteers happy to share wisdom harvested over many growing seasons. You can always start small and grow from there.

Gardening also offers the chance to spend busy but peaceful time outdoors. A 2022 study in the journal *Urban Forestry and Urban Greening* suggests that the hobby of gardening reinforces your connection to nature and helps relieve stress. In the study, the authors noted that during times of uncertainty in the world "in gardens and gardening people may still find a sense of hope."[11]

Woodworking

Making a hobby of woodworking means you might make furniture, canoes, birdhouses, picture frames, or any of countless other items to enjoy yourself, give to others, or sell. Woodworking is often a hobby passed down from one generation to the next, but even if you don't have a parent or grandparent who's handy with a saw and a sander, you can be the first in your family to develop this rewarding pastime.

Among the challenges of woodworking are that it does require a variety of tools, some of which can be expensive, and it requires the space to work on your projects. You can sometimes find good deals on tools online, at yard sales, or in thrift stores. Some shops that repair power tools also sell used items, so don't hesitate to call around to see what's available in your community. You won't need every tool to begin—there are about seven or eight basic starter items—so do some research before investing in your tools of the trade. Woodworking also requires care and skill to avoid injury, so if possible, try to work with a more experienced craftsperson or get some supervised instruction first.

You might want to take woodshop in school if the course is offered. That's how Dos Pueblos High School (California) student Zander Doherty got his start in woodworking—a hobby that led

Woodworking requires more specialized equipment and supplies than some hobbies, but it can be very rewarding for people who enjoy hands-on work.

him to a Best in Show and People's Choice Award at the 2023 Association of Woodworkers & Furnishings Suppliers national competition. He signed up for woodshop in seventh grade. "I had originally thought that we would simply be given a chisel and a mallet and would be carving," says Doherty. "To my surprise, the shop was full of power tools and after building a couple small projects, I soon realized that I loved woodworking and I haven't stopped building since."[12] While the number of schools offering these courses dipped during the 1990s and early 2000s, in recent years more schools are reintroducing vocational classes like woodshop, metal shop, automotive repair, and other hands-on programs.

> **"I soon realized that I loved woodworking and I haven't stopped building since."[12]**
>
> —Zander Doherty, high school student and national woodworking award winner

Other Hands-On Hobbies

The attraction of hands-on hobbies is that you can enjoy both the process and the finished product. Building model vehicles or detailed dioramas allows you to focus on precision work while giving you something tangible to appreciate at the end. Maybe you loved LEGO bricks as a kid and want to start snapping pieces together again to create skyscrapers or space stations requiring thousands of pieces.

Try your hand at making soap, candles, or other items that can be useful when you're done. Crocheting, knitting, and sewing can be relaxing, while allowing you to be creative and produce something that someone will wear, knowing it was made with skill and affection. There's almost no end to what you can make or repair with your imagination, problem-solving skills, and hands.

Keep Your Brain Busy

While every hobby requires a certain amount of decision-making, planning, and other cognitive skills, there are certain pastimes that really challenge the brain and open your mind up to new worlds and new ways of thinking. There is a lot of research suggesting that along with simply fueling your knowledge and passion for a subject you find interesting, brain-boosting hobbies do promote better memory and thinking skills throughout your life. For example, a 2023 study in the journal *Psychological Medicine* suggested that teenagers who spend at least twelve hours a week reading for pleasure tend to get higher test scores and enjoy better mental health. And a 2012 study in the *Spanish Journal of Psychology* found that kids who play chess regularly experience improvements in coping and problem-solving skills.

Of course, you can read, play chess, and do other brain-boosting hobbies just for fun. And within this category are plenty of activities you can enjoy on your own for some quiet downtime or share with others who like the same things.

Reading

For Long Beach (California) high school student Selene Velez, a love of reading became more than just a hobby when she decided to share her passion for books with others on TikTok. It didn't take long for her to develop a following of younger kids who enjoyed videos of her reading and recommending books. The Mexican Filipina teenager told *ABC7 Eyewitness News* that she was particularly excited about highlighting the work of authors who share her cultural identity. "As a person with a platform [I try] to give spotlight to people who have my similar background, just to kind of raise up our voices and also relate to other content creators and hype each other up," she said, adding that her main message is to encourage kids to keep reading. "Even if it's small, take the time. Five minutes, *cinco minutos*; please spend some time reading."[13]

To make reading less of a solitary hobby, join or start a book club with some friends. Members can all read the same book at the same time and meet regularly to talk about the latest chapters they've read. Or club members can share and recommend books they've enjoyed or attend readings by visiting authors in the community. Your local library may sponsor a book club or other reading events, too.

Many people are passionate about reading. Some people are solitary readers; others prefer to make the activity more social by starting or joining a book club.

If reading is more of a solitary hobby, think about doing so with a bigger or long-term goal in mind. Perhaps try reading all the books written by a particular author or focusing on a particular historical or cultural subject and learning as much as you can about that topic.

Writing

If you have a story to tell, have a poem to share, or just want to get your thoughts and feelings down on paper, then writing can be the perfect hobby for you. Berkeley High School (California) senior Lincoln Roan started writing poetry after being inspired by a friend who loved to write. In the fall of 2023, Roan told his high school paper, the *Berkeley High Jacket*, "I feel when you share writing that's coming from your heart and your lived experiences, people can find relatability in that. And they can also find, 'oh my god, this is a way that I can express how I'm feeling.' It's an emotional outlet, which is a very important thing to have in your life."[14]

Writing can take many forms, too. If you love movies, try writing a screenplay. There are inexpensive computer programs you can download that will automatically format your screenplay as you write. Maybe you can start a blog about study strategies, stress management, or your favorite movies, TV series, or music. You may want to simply journal your ideas, observations, and experiences. If you'd like to write about other subjects but aren't sure where to start, you can find countless writing prompts online or in journals. Journaling prompts or activities include things like five minutes of free expression or stream-of-consciousness thoughts. You might also write a fictional dialogue between yourself and someone you know. Other popular ideas include scribbling a cartoon; making lists of favorite activities, movies, or songs; or expressing your feelings in rhyme or free verse. "Journaling activities can be designed to help young people gain insights into the major areas of their lives—including relationships with peers, parents and other adults, their bodies and health issues, and careers and other special interests,"[15] says Lynn Pike, a sociology professor at the University of Missouri.

> **"Journaling activities can be designed to help young people gain insights into the major areas of their lives."[15]**
>
> **—Lynn Pike, University of Missouri sociology professor**

You might find that writing in a nice, hardbound blank journal helps inspire you, though you can be just as creative and expressive writing in a spiral notebook or on your laptop. Keep in mind that writing can be something that you do for yourself or that you do hoping to find an audience, even if that means your friends and family. And the more you write and the more comfortable you are sharing your work with others, the more motivated you might be to try something ambitious, like a novel. Until then, try to enjoy the process of writing and the feedback you get from others about what you have to say and just how you say it.

Astronomy

When the sun has set and you've finished dinner and your homework, consider stepping outside to study the moon and stars. Lucy Will, a high school student in Honolulu, Hawaii, turned her early fascination with astronomy into a research project that was accepted for publication in the *Research Notes of the American Astronomical Society* in 2022. She was mentored by two University of Hawaii professors, who guided her research into the size and intensity of sunspots. She told University of Hawai'i News:

> When I was young, I used to love gazing up into the night sky and imagining everything that lay beyond our own planet. What did it look like out there? I stared for hours at pictures of the Pillars of Creation, Saturn and Neptune. I was hooked. The idea of being able to make new discoveries by working on my own project was super exciting. I absolutely loved the whole process—learning to code,

working with the data, finally seeing the results we were looking for, and eventually writing the research note! I am so grateful that I had the opportunity to be introduced into this field and I am looking forward to many more projects in the future![16]

You don't need a fancy, expensive telescope to get started. With the naked eye you can learn a lot about the landmarks on the moon and various constellations. And with a simple pair of binoculars, you get an even better look at the details of the lunar surface, as well as planets, star clusters, and other objects in the night sky. If your interest in astronomy grows, then you can shop around for a telescope. Look for online reviews of telescopes for beginners and check out yard sales or thrift stores that might have secondhand telescopes ready to be pointed at the stars again.

Telescopes are useful tools for astronomy hobbyists, but they are not essential. You can observe many celestial objects with binoculars or even with the naked eye.

And on nights when the weather isn't cooperating, you can explore the galaxy through books, magazines, and websites, such as Space.com and *Sky & Telescope*, or visit a planetarium in your community.

Chess

Chess has long been a game played by people who enjoy the mental challenge of trying to stay a few moves ahead of an opponent. The Netflix series *The Queen's Gambit* brought mainstream attention to the game. And opportunities to learn chess and compete against others around the world through Chess.com, Lichess (for younger kids), and other digital chess games have drastically boosted interest in recent years. The first step is to learn the rules of chess—how the board is set up to start each game, how each piece moves, and how to win. Chess is maybe the ultimate strategy game, so learning some basic strategies and how to anticipate your opponent's game plan will serve you well the longer you play.

Making Your Hobby a Habit

You want to start a new hobby, but between school, a part-time job, and other obligations, you're struggling to find the time or motivation to commit to it. Maybe you're a procrastinator or you just have trouble setting a schedule or getting started with any project. It's not a lost cause. To help make a hobby a habit, try to pick something you can do with a friend or a group. Choose an activity that others enjoy, so that you can keep each other motivated and be accountable to one another. You'll be less likely to skip an afternoon yoga workout if your best friend is waiting for you at the gym. Hobbies that involve a set schedule, such as after-school meetings or rehearsals, also can be easier to stick with because they have consistent start and stop times on the same days each week. You can make them a part of your schedule the way you would with school, work, or other responsibilities. The other strategy is to start small. Taking on too much at first can be overwhelming and cause you to quit. And remember that the more frequently you do something, the more likely it is to become a habit.

In the 2020 Netflix miniseries The Queen's Gambit, *a young prodigy skyrockets through the ranks to become a chess superstar.*

If you're considering chess, remember that it is a game for everybody, no matter how old you are or what your grades are, explains Maurice Ashley, the first Black individual to earn the title of Grandmaster (the top designation in the world of chess) from the International Chess Federation. In a 2023 interview with *Education Week*, Ashley said, "It's just a game; that's the beauty of it. It's a game structured so you can't help but think about your plans, and what the other person's plans are. That's the great debate that takes place on the board."[17] He recommends that kids who want to start playing and improve their skills try to play at least twice a week for forty-five minutes at a time.

Puzzles

In a digital world, pastimes as simple and old-school as jigsaw puzzles and crossword puzzles may seem too old-fashioned to be embraced by young people. But that's not the case at all. In 2020, when COVID-19 kept everyone home for months on end, sales of jigsaw puzzles shot up by more than 300 percent as

How Colleges Look at Hobbies

While grades, test scores, and other academic achievements may get most of the attention from college admissions officers, don't underestimate how much an interesting hobby might impress them, too. Yes, colleges want successful, well-rounded students, but they also want outstanding ones, people who will bring unique gifts and experiences to campus. That's not to say you should take up an obscure hobby just to set your application apart. Instead, feel free to share your sincere interests and passions as part of your application, especially if they're a little different. Are you and your parents amateur beekeepers? Have you been juggling since you were seven years old? Do you and your best friend have a horror movie podcast? Alix Coupet, a former college admissions officer at Stanford University, recommends that you "lean into your weirdness" and share your hobbies, why they're important to you, and what you've learned from them. "Admissions counselors are human and if 100 kids say the same thing we can get a little tired of mundane stories. And so we are looking for stories that are going to be distinctive."

Quoted in Abigail Johnson Hess, "Former Stanford Admissions Officer: 'Well-Rounded Is Not Enough'—Here's How to Really Stand Out," CNBC, October 22, 2021. www.cnbc.com.

families sought ways to stay occupied and reduce the stress of lockdowns. But puzzling has always had its share of enthusiasts before and since the pandemic's early impact.

For University of Kentucky student Michaela Keener, it was growing up in northern Minnesota that inspired an appreciation and passion for jigsaw puzzles. She became so good at completing complex puzzles quickly that she qualified for the World Jigsaw Puzzle Championships in 2023. "I've been puzzling my whole life," she told the University of Kentucky News in 2023. "But I'm from Northern Minnesota, so you spend a lot of time in the winter inside with not much to do—unless you want to read or puzzle."[18]

Jigsaw puzzles are sold in department stores, in toy stores, and online, with puzzles ranging from a few dozen pieces for kids to several hundred pieces or more than one thousand pieces for the more competitive puzzlers (five-hundred-piece puzzles are often used at speed competitions). Consider starting puzzles as a hobby the next time the weather keeps you indoors or you just need to unplug, concentrate, and relax with something quiet. And if you're concerned that putting together a jigsaw puzzle is just a mindless pursuit, just know that a Yale University study found that working with others on jigsaw puzzles improves your short-term memory and problem-solving skills and gives you a rewarding sense of collaboration. And you can always use special puzzle glue to preserve the final product after you put the last piece in place.

Crossword puzzles can also be done in collaboration or on your own. And you can find simple puzzles in books or online, or you can try more challenging versions, like the famous *New York Times* crossword puzzle. Crossword puzzles challenge your brain by having you solve word-play riddles, recall historical and scientific facts, and keep up with current trends and pop culture to solve all of the clues. And if you're especially ambitious, you can elevate the hobby of solving problems to one in which you create the puzzles. For Garrett Chalfin, an eighteen-year-old senior at New York City's Riverdale Country School in 2023, a crossword-crafting hobby led to having one of his puzzles accepted for publication in the Sunday *New York Times*. The feat made him something of a celebrity among his friends, who were also crossword fanatics, while also fulfilling a goal he'd had for years as a crossword hobbyist. "It's just a really nice hobby because it's creative and I'm working my brain simultaneously. And also you produce something,"[19] he said in a 2023 article in *New York* magazine.

"[Creating crossword puzzles is] just a really nice hobby because it's creative and I'm working my brain simultaneously."[19]

—Garrett Chalfin, high school senior

Keep Your Brain Busy

Hobbies are meant to be enjoyable breaks from school, work, and other responsibilities. That doesn't mean you can't engage in a hobby that challenges your thinking skills. Aside from keeping you entertained, brain-boosting hobbies can help improve memory and thinking skills—now and in the future.

High-Tech Hobbies

Computer-based hobbies can include something for just about anyone's interests, such as designing video games, programming robots, making movies, and creating smartphone apps. If you're comfortable using technology and have an interest in learning more about the power of computing, think about the many high-tech hobbies that are out there.

Tech-based hobbies can be fun and rewarding pursuits on their own. Building a robot as part of a team can create lasting memories and forge new friendships. The same is true for creating a video game or making a short animated film on your computer. But for some people, what started as a hobby became a successful career. In an article he wrote for Medium, a collaborative website for writers, Orhun Dalabasmaz wrote about how he and his older brother enjoyed building computers, in large part to play video games, after an uncle gave them their family's first computer. "After a while, we started collecting computer pieces one by one," he wrote. "We both saved the money and bought one piece at a time."[20] Today Dalabasmaz is a successful computer engineer with the international tech company Atlassian.

Coding

Many tech-based hobbies require the ability to code, or program a computer to perform certain tasks. Fortunately, there are countless online tutorials, books, and other resources to help you learn. Many communities have after-school coding clubs or summer coding camps for kids. That's how a group of Northern California teens spent part of their summer vacation in 2023—at a three-week App Development Summer Camp at Columbia College. Among them was Summerville High School student Austin Auld, who wanted to finally learn how to code after spending years being curious about it. "It's always fascinated me," Auld said in a 2023 article in the Sonora, California, *Union Democrat*. "I've messed around with code before but this is my first chance to study it. It's a chance to create things, create movement, and create artificial life."[21]

You don't need a summer camp or a school club to get into coding. There is no shortage of online videos, tutorials, and other resources to help beginners or anyone with a little experience in programming. Learning to code allows you to create computer games, design apps, and work on web design and development. You can take your newfound coding skills and put them toward your interests. If you're an athlete, you might want to create an app to track your training and performances, for example. Or you may just want to create games you and your friends can play together.

> **"Once I learned how to code, I realized that I actually got very similar enjoyment from [coding] that I got from video games."[22]**
>
> **—Grant Darling, software developer**

Software developer Grant Darling, whose blog is called *The Code Bytes*, suggests that kids who learn to code as a hobby may find they enjoy it just as much as any video game. He writes:

> When I was a kid, I used to spend way too much time playing video games. Once I learned how to code, I realized that I actually got very similar enjoyment from [coding] that I got from video games. The only difference was that coding was much more challenging than most games I played. So the highs I get from coding are much less frequent than from a video game. However, they were also much more rewarding![22]

Robotics

Whirring motors, swinging mechanical arms, and screaming teenagers? The annual FIRST Robotics Competition, which features student-built robots engaging in a variety of tasks inside an arena, draws more than eighty thousand students from dozens of countries to robotics events all year long. The competitions—which have robots toss traffic cones onto poles, shoot rubber balls through hoops, stack objects, or attempt other sporting challenges—take on the atmosphere of high-stakes basketball games, with kids cheering wildly for their teams to come out on top.

Robots, which used to be limited to science-fiction stories or far-fetched predictions of life in the future, are at the heart of a rapidly growing hobby for teens and younger children today. You can find robotics kits online or in many hobby stores and electronics stores. And schools around the world are sponsoring robotics clubs—many of which dream of competing internationally. The nonprofit group For Inspiration and Recognition of Science and Technology (FIRST) sponsors the biggest robotics competitions in the

Robots built by high school students go head-to-head at a FIRST Robotics Competition in Long Beach, California, on March 26, 2010.

world, partnering in some contests with LEGO, which sells robotics kits for a range of skill levels. Bogue Chitto School (Mississippi) student Caroline Jordan, part of her school's robotics team called the Technocats, says the camaraderie among her teammates and competitors is part of what makes robotics so fun. "At competitions you realize you are all nerds," Jordan said in a 2023 interview with the Brookhaven, Mississippi, *Daily Leader* newspaper. "My brother was in the LEGO League and introduced me to LEGOs. I eventually learned you can do bigger stuff in robotics and I love it. At competitions, we are like one big family."[23]

> **"I eventually learned you can do bigger stuff in robotics and I love it. At competitions, we are like one big family."[23]**
>
> **—Caroline Jordan, Mississippi high school student**

Even if you don't pursue the competitive side of robotics, you can still enjoy it as a hobby you do on your own or with a few friends or family members. Robotics combines coding and construction. You'll need some basic tools to put robots together—ones you either buy in a kit or build on your own—and some programming knowledge. But robotics, like so many high-tech hobbies, is one you can learn as you go. The fun is in the learning and the doing as well as the finished product.

Digital Art and Animation

Being interested in computers and technology doesn't mean you can't also have artistic pursuits. Digital art and animation allow you to express your ideas using the tools with which you're comfortable. There are 2-D and 3-D animation software programs available, though 2-D may be an easier way to learn what it takes to create moving characters and interesting settings. Animation software is getting less expensive, and you may find free software you can download to get you started.

Keep in mind, though, that your first animations aren't going to look like the latest Pixar masterpiece. However, if you have a knack for it, Hollywood may come calling. What started as a

Video Games as a Lucrative Hobby

You might spend hours playing video games alone, with friends next to you on the couch, or with distant players online. But you might not have ever considered it a hobby in the same way that collecting action figures or crocheting or painting water colors is a hobby. Yet if a hobby is, at its core, an activity you do regularly for fun during your leisure time, then playing *Minecraft*, *Mario Kart*, *Rocket League*, *Animal Crossing*, and the rest could be considered great hobbies. To make your gaming feel more like a hobby and less like a study break or merely a way to pass the time, think about competitive gaming, known as esports. If you get good enough at certain games, you can earn prize money and even college scholarships. Nearly two hundred colleges and universities have esports programs, many of which offer tuition scholarships. "For us, it's really nice to be able to offer that scholarship opportunity for them to be able to come here and not only get their education but continue doing something they love," says Northern Kentucky University esports director Shanda Harris.

Quoted in Jasmine Styles, "His Parents Were Concerned He Was Playing Video Games Too Much. Then It Started Paying for His Tuition," WCPO, August 24, 2022. www.wcpo.com.

hobby making short, animated films on his computer landed a Toronto teen with an assignment to create a segment in the blockbuster 2023 film *Spider-Man: Across the Spider-Verse*. Preston Mutanga, age fourteen, captured the attention of *Spider-Man* filmmakers Chris Miller and Phil Lord with a shot-for-shot homemade LEGO-inspired remake of the trailer for the 2018 *Spider-Man: Into the Spider-Verse* he posted on YouTube. "We found out that it was a 14-year-old kid who made it and we were like, 'This looks incredibly sophisticated for a non-adult, nonprofessional to have made,'" Miller told the *New York Times*. "It blew us all away, including some of the best animators in the world."[24] Mutanga was later hired to make a short LEGO-themed scene for the sequel. But like so many hobbyists, he started out just having fun with something that captured his attention and inspired his imagination. "My dad showed me this 3-D software called Blender and I instantly got hooked on it," he told the *Los Angeles Times*. "I watched a lot of YouTube videos to teach myself certain stuff."[25]

And if your interests lean more toward paintings or illustrations, rather than moving images, digital art can be a computer-based hobby to pursue. You'll need a drawing tablet and stylus to get started, along with illustration and drawing apps or computer programs. These range from sophisticated software used by professionals to those suited for beginners.

If your academic interests lie in science, math, and engineering, digital art can be one way to keep you in the world of technology as you express yourself creatively. Huda Warsame, a member of Michigan's Wayne State University School of Medicine Class of 2025, wants a career in medicine. But she hasn't given up on hobbies that help her manage stress and pursue her art. "I think a part of keeping well in medical school is having and keeping

Hobbyists who want to combine their artistic talents with technology may enjoy digital art and animation, which involves creating images using computers.

“I try to continue with my painting and digital art since being in school. I find it as a good way to unwind and to also work the more creative/artistic side of my brain.”[26]

—Huda Warsame, Wayne State University medical student

up with your hobbies,” she told Wayne State University School of Medicine News in 2023. “I try to continue with my painting and digital art since being in school. I find it as a good way to unwind and to also work the more creative/artistic side of my brain.”[26]

3-D Printing

3-D printing is a manufacturing process that takes a digital file (design) and creates a three-dimensional, tangible object from that file. These can include toys, pieces of art, useful household items, or just about anything, depending on the sophistication of the printer and the software it uses. The main piece of equipment is a 3-D printer, which can range in price from about $300 for a basic desktop model to more than $2,000 (sometimes much more) for a large printer capable of creating more complex objects.

Have a Hobby, Start a Club

One of the most fun parts of having a hobby can be sharing it with others. But you may not know other kids who also like launching rockets or making movies or any other activity that you enjoy. If your school has a club devoted to a hobby of yours, consider joining, even if you don’t know any of the other members or are a little introverted—not usually a “joiner.” Unlike in a lot of social situations, you already know you have something in common with other kids in a hobby club. And most people who have a real interest in any subject are usually welcoming of others who like the same things. And if your school has no club based on a hobby you enjoy, consider starting one. Usually, you just need a teacher or administrator to be a club sponsor and a space to meet. Some schools may even provide funds if you need equipment of some kind. Posters or announcements at school or on the school’s website may be enough to attract fellow rocketeers, filmmakers, knitters, or book lovers to form a new community right in your own school.

3-D printing is an expensive and sometimes tricky hobby, requiring lots of trial and error, but mastering it can be very satisfying.

3-D printing requires design software and "slicing" software, which takes your design and creates a file made up of hundreds or thousands of digital layers or slices. Your printer creates objects one layer at a time. You will also need the materials for your creations—usually some type of plastic, but 3-D printers can also make objects out of foam, metal, and other materials.

As cool as 3-D printing is, it can also be a challenging hobby. Expect a lot of trial and error. In a 2022 article for *Wired* magazine, Kenneth R. Rosen shared advice about getting started in 3-D printing as a teenager, using his own early efforts as examples of why patience and realistic expectations about the printer's capability and your own skills are so important. He suggests that beginners not get caught up in getting an expensive printer with all the "bells and whistles." Learn as you go and expect that your first prints may not look quite like you envisioned them in the design phase. "Take those first prints for what they are: learning experiences," he wrote. "With practice will eventually come mastery, at which point the upgrades and bells and whistles will make more sense and bring you greater satisfaction and reward."[27]

Other High-Tech Hobbies

Computer-based hobby options really run the gamut from serious to silly. You may have a passion for history, for example. Taking free online history courses may seem like more schooling at first, but if the classes support a subject that you simply enjoy learning about, then take them. Conversely, you may enjoy teaching others about a subject you like. Start a YouTube channel and let others with the same interests find you online. Of course, you may prefer a YouTube channel composed entirely of funny videos you and your friends make.

Or think about starting a podcast with a friend or a group of friends. Four high school friends and sports fans from East Brunswick, New Jersey, were hanging out one night and decided to start a sports podcast. "We did a lot of research and found that Spotify was a really easy way for us to start up a podcast," Rohan Patel told the online newspaper My Central Jersey in 2023. "So, we were like, 'Alright, let's try this. Let's see where it goes.'"[28] They've since produced dozens of episodes and interviewed professional athletes.

For any online hobbies you pursue—whether they're games, courses, videos, podcasts, or simply emailing experts for advice—make sure your parents or guardians know what's going on. Technology can open so many worlds, but it's important to be cautious about who you let into yours.

CHAPTER FOUR

Hobbies and the Arts

From the time you were very young, you probably spent many contented hours drawing, playacting, singing, or otherwise expressing yourself creatively. That creative side of you is probably still there waiting to be rediscovered. And the great thing about an artistic hobby is that it can be as personal or as public as you want.

If you've always wanted to play guitar, you can take lessons and strum away for hours on your own or join a band and share your new skills with friends who want to play the same kind of music. The same is true for your watercolors, sculptures, photographs, dancing, and more. Create things for you to enjoy or to share with others. Creative hobbies do more than let you express your ideas and artistic visions. The arts give you a chance to make something lasting, whether it's the memory of a meaningful performance or something tangible, like a piece of pottery or a painting.

The arts are usually categorized as visual arts (such as painting, pottery making, and photography) and performing arts (such as playing an instrument, singing, dancing, and acting). Just remember, you don't have to be a world-class artist or dancer to make any of these hobbies a lot of fun. And for many people, the arts are the path to lasting friendships. For Jack Riley, a computer science major at Brown University, a love of playing music that started out as a high school hobby became more meaningful once he got to college. "I've met most of my closest friends through bands and music classes,"[29] he told the *Brown Daily Herald* in 2023.

Learning a Musical Instrument

In 2020 and 2021 an estimated 16 million Americans began to play guitar, according to a study conducted by Fender, one of the leading guitar makers in the world. Of those new guitarists, nearly three-fourths were ages thirteen to thirty-four. While the COVID-19 pandemic certainly contributed to the surge in six-string music makers, the reality is that every year brings forth a new wave of young people strumming their hearts out with acoustic and electric guitars. Along with people picking up a guitar for the first time, every year also sees new generations of pianists, trumpet players, drummers, and other first-time musicians discovering the joys of playing music.

Learning to play an instrument can be both fun and frustrating. But as Nebraska high school musician Morgan Lahm wrote in *Teen Magazine* in 2022, making mistakes and learning from them are good lessons for life and for improving your musicianship. "It can be tricky to love something you aren't good at yet," Lahm said. "Once you are better at playing your instrument, you will hopefully develop a passion for it, which is a huge stepping stone in your musical growth."[30]

> **"It can be tricky to love something you aren't good at yet. Once you are better at playing your instrument, you will hopefully develop a passion for it, which is a huge stepping stone in your musical growth."[30]**
>
> —Morgan Lahm, Nebraska high school student musician

Deciding what instrument to play comes down to several factors, such as what instruments are easily accessible, their cost, and your personal interests. If you want to learn how to play your favorite songs on guitar or piano (or keyboard), then the choice is easy. However, learning to play an instrument requires consistent practice, so if you don't have a guitar, piano, or other instrument available on a regular basis, you'll need to either buy or borrow one first. You can find beginners' guitars and electric keyboards for under $100, though as the quality of the instrument goes up, so does the price.

Learning to play a musical instrument is time-consuming and requires a great deal of practice—but the effort brings great rewards that last a lifetime.

While you may learn and advance more quickly with one-on-one instruction, you can also teach yourself to play by watching videos and taking online music instruction classes. But the key, as with most skills, is practice, practice, practice.

If you want to play in your school orchestra or band, then you may want to find out what instruments are available from your school or where you can rent an instrument locally. Joining the beginning band in your school can be a great way to launch your music hobby because you'll be doing so alongside other new musicians. It's also a way to be exposed to several different instruments. If you start out on the trombone but really like the sound of the saxophone, for example, you can always change your instrument.

And just like most kids who play sports will never play in college or the pros, most kids who play a musical instrument will also never make music a career. But it can be a hobby you enjoy your whole life.

Get Your Friends Dancing as a DJ

If you have ever been to a dance or party and seen a DJ wearing headphones and standing behind a computer, turntables, and sound system, you may have wondered what it takes to do that. Being a DJ used to involve little more than playing records and chatting a little in between songs. But in recent years DJs have become some of the biggest stars in the international music scene. DJs make a living keeping the music and energy going at events that range from small weddings to huge festivals. But being a DJ can also be a fun hobby, just playing locally. To get started, you'll need a computer and DJ software that allows you to mix songs. You'll also need actual song files. You can download them (which can add up if you're paying per song) or subscribe to a DJ pool, which allows unlimited downloads. Port Huron, Michigan, teenager Gunner Welch started DJing as a hobby and enjoyed it so much that he turned it into a part-time job, working weddings, school dances, and even the Port Huron Chilly Fest. "You know, this is quite fun, why not try and make a little money off it?" he told the *Detroit News*.

Quoted in Jeremy Ervin, "Teen DJ Turns Hobby into Job," *Detroit News*, January 28, 2019. www.detroitnews.com.

Singing

Kelly Clarkson is one of the most successful singers of her generation, but she says she never really thought her voice was anything special while growing up. In an interview on her talk show in 2020, she admitted that in her small town she was surrounded by family members and friends who sang a lot, especially in church. She assumed everyone could carry a tune, and most of her friends seemed to have better voices than she had. In the seventh grade, though, her school's chorus teacher overheard her and encouraged Clarkson to join the program. After performing in some high school musicals and trying unsuccessfully to break into the music business right after high school, Clarkson auditioned for *American Idol* at age twenty, and, well, superstardom followed.

Whether you have undiscovered talent or just like to belt out a tune now and then, singing can be a rewarding hobby. Research shows that singing boosts your mood because it activates multiple parts of the brain (more than simply speaking does) and it leads to the release of "feel good" brain chemicals called endorphins.

Like most skills, singing can usually improve with practice and a little instruction. Take music classes at school or join the chorus; sometimes singing with others at first helps ease any nervousness you might have about singing publicly. Taking private lessons with a vocal coach may give you more confidence, too, while honing your music skills. "Ever since I was young, I have loved singing," says Payton Riley, a fourteen-year-old aspiring country singer from Texas. "I would go around the house screaming at the top of my lungs and so my mom was, like, one day, 'Would you like to do singing lessons to get some of that energy out?'"[31]

You never know. If singing doesn't lead to a career in music, you can still enjoy performing in choruses, choirs, a cappella groups, musical theater, or even your car as the radio plays.

Singer Kelly Clarkson, who turned her singing hobby into a profession after winning season one of the TV show American Idol, *performs in New York City on September 22, 2023.*

Dancing

Dancing is a hobby enjoyed by people of all ages, skill levels, and tastes in music. You can dance to hip hop, jazz, show tunes, Latin music, and classical waltzes, and that's just for starters. Dance offers a good workout while also being a way to express yourself and unwind to music you love. And because dance is usually something enjoyed in a group setting, it can also be a way to make friends and shake off any hesitancy about meeting new people. "I was a very shy child," says Tulsa teen Anna Gatz, who joined the Oklahoma Swing Syndicate after accompanying her family to swing dances at her church. "After I started swing dancing, I kind of bloomed. I would have lots of different people come and dance with me, and I had to talk to them. So it really brought me out of my shell."[32]

> "After I started swing dancing, I kind of bloomed."[32]
>
> —Anna Gatz, Oklahoma teen dancer

Formal dance lessons are the best way to learn, and they are usually taught in group sessions for beginners. Try to convince a friend or family member to join you, but if that's not possible, remember that a class for beginners is just that—a group of people learning the same way you are.

Magic

When Dennis Kim was about ten years old, his older brother charged into his room with a few dollar bills in his hand. After Kim's brother let go of the bills, they remained suspended in the air. It was the first magic trick Kim remembers seeing close-up, and it changed everything for the young New Yorker, who has gone on to make a career of fooling audiences in the same way. "I remember as a kid, distinctly, it was a feeling I had never felt before," Kim told CNBC Make It in 2022. "Of being fooled and really fascinated, astonished that something like that could happen in front of my eyes. . . . It instantly became the hobby that took most of my time."[33]

Calling All Collectors

One of the most common hobbies for people of any age is collecting. Chances are you or someone in your family already has a collection of items such as coins, wind chimes, comic books, old video games, or other items that make you smile just to look at, listen to, or otherwise enjoy. Part of the fun of having a collection is displaying it so that you are surrounded by things that bring you joy or revisiting your collectibles from time to time, whether they're in scrapbooks or boxes. But an even bigger thrill can sometimes be found in the search for new additions to your collection. And when friends or relatives know you're on the hunt for a hard-to-find item, discovering that prize and giving it as a gift can be just as exciting for them as it is for you. Collecting is also a hobby that you can do for just a few minutes a week or a few hours. Just keep in mind that collecting can be an expensive hobby, especially if you're gathering rare items like old baseball cards or vintage dolls. You'll also need space for your collection, so consider those things before you become a collector.

Even if you don't become a professional magician like Kim, you can still perform magic tricks for friends and audiences as a hobby. Magic trick sets can be purchased in toy stores, hobby stores, and bookstores as well as online. And even though magicians aren't supposed to reveal their secrets, you can find no shortage of magicians doing just that with YouTube videos or online tutorials

Drawing and Painting

You've probably been drawing and painting since before you can remember. You may still have some of your early work, with a smiling sun in the corner of the paper looking down on your stick-figure family. Even if your artistic skills haven't improved much, drawing and painting can still be fun and relaxing hobbies—whether you're painting on canvas or detailing tiny tabletop gaming figures.

Alyssa Garcia, a student at Austin Peay State University in Tennessee, initially turned to painting miniature figurines as a stress-relieving hobby during her freshman year. But she found that her artistic endeavors also gave her a nice self-esteem boost and a sense of accomplishment. "When you finish one and it ends up looking nice it definitely feels good. Like a sense of pride,"[34] Garcia told her college paper the *All State*.

Before you invest heavily in art supplies, especially if you're a beginner, think about what medium you prefer. In painting, your main options are acrylics, oils, and watercolors. Acrylics are easy to use as well as versatile, meaning they can be easily blended and used on many different surfaces. The one downside is that they dry quickly, so if you are hoping to mix your colors, you'll have to work fast. Watercolors, which are usually the most affordable paints, also tend to dry quickly. And because they are water based and very "flowy," watercolors can often run on the paper.

Of course, in addition to paint, you'll need the brushes that are best suited for the type of paint you choose, an easel, paint, and paper or canvas, again depending on your medium of choice. The more you pursue painting, the more tools you might need, such as palettes, palette knives, thinners, and brush cleaners.

Whether you have professional-level artistic skills or can barely manage stick figures, drawing and painting can be very enjoyable creative outlets.

Cartooning, sketching, and other types of drawing may require fewer supplies, but there are countless types of pens and pencils you can use. Drawing thicker or finer lines or ones with darker or lighter tones all require a variety of implements. And don't forget a good pencil eraser and paper or a sketchbook.

Pottery Making

Pottery making as a hobby can involve having clay, a potter's wheel, kiln, and other equipment in your home, though many people who want to make it a hobby rely on pottery studios in their community. You may want to look around at studios that offer classes or are open to anyone interested in making their own clay pots, bowls, mugs, plates, or other items. But once you start and get the hang of it, you may be hooked for life. Venice High School (California) student Imogen Rosenberg regularly drops in on Good Dirt LA, a pottery studio near her home, after her school stopped offering pottery classes. She says pottery is a creative outlet and a stress relieverer at the same time. The nice thing is that the finished product doesn't have to look a particular way or meet a particular standard. "In pottery you can let your mind run free," she wrote in her school's paper, the *Oarsmen.* "You don't have to worry about things being perfect. Just think about your hands on the clay."[35]

> **"In pottery you can let your mind run free. You don't have to worry about things being perfect."[35]**
>
> —Imogen Rosenberg, California high school student and pottor

Photography

As cameras in smartphones have gotten progressively more sophisticated and capable of producing beautiful pictures and videos, billions of people around the world have become photographers of sorts. But to turn picture taking into a real hobby, you'll need to produce more than selfies and other random images. While you can still use a smartphone and its many camera features to develop your photographer's eye, you may eventually want to move up to a more traditional digital camera. A basic camera with a simple zoom lens can be purchased for under $100, but for more advanced models that will allow you to shoot a great variety of subjects, expect to pay several hundred dollars. These are called digital single-lens reflex, or DSLR, cameras, and most photographers suggest that beginners invest in them over simple point-and-shoot cameras that aren't really better than what's in your phone.

Look online or at pawn shops for used cameras to save a little money at the outset. When you're ready to edit your photos, even if it's just sizing and cropping, as opposed to applying artistic filters and other touches, free and low-cost photo-editing programs and apps are readily available. Unlike film cameras from years ago, digital cameras don't require pricey rolls of film. You will need memory cards, but you can find versatile and long-lasting cards for $30 to $300.

Photography has several other advantages, too. It helps you find beauty in the world and document your life's journey while preserving old and new memories along the way. Photography is also accessible to just about everyone, regardless of any disability or other factor that might make pursuing other hobbies more difficult. And photography allows you to shoot pictures just for yourself as well as to share with others. You might enter your photos in contests, take pictures for your school yearbook, or find some other way to let others see what you see through the lens of your camera.

How the Arts May Change You

A hobby in the arts provides a way to tap into your creative side. It can be a vehicle for expressing your feelings and ideas—for your own enjoyment or as a way to speak to others. Whether you pursue hobbies in visual arts or performing arts, those pastimes are likely to show you new ways to look at yourself and the world around you.

Time to Get Active

If you're looking for a hobby that will also give you a good workout, you might want to try sports or other recreational activities that get your heart pumping and your muscles moving. You don't need to limit yourself to organized sports. Bicycling, rock climbing, and running can be hobbies that take you around your community or around the world. Active hobbies are also great choices because they can be done with lots of other people, just a few friends, or even on your own if you want a break from the crowd.

When thinking about making a sport or other athletic pursuit a hobby, keep in mind the physical demands of that activity and how your body, fitness level, experiences, and abilities line up with those demands. Long-distance running, for example, requires a level of cardiovascular fitness beyond that required for skateboarding or golf. At the same time, if you are determined to take up running, then be patient and careful as your capacity improves with every run.

It's also worth noting that if you rely on a wheelchair or are visually impaired or face other challenges to traditional sports and physical activities, there are ever-expanding opportunities to participate in adapted athletics. Marcus Onsum, executive director of the Minnesota Adapted Athletics Association, has been part of the movement to open up sports to more young people who want to enjoy active hobbies but have limited physical abilities. "By the time they get to us, it's just been one obstacle after another. 'No, no, no, no, no, you can't do this.' And when we finally say, 'Yes, you can do this, you can play soccer, you can play hockey, you

Physical impairments are no barrier to athletic hobbies, thanks to specialized equipment that allows athletes of all abilities to participate.

can play softball. It's just going to look a little different than what you're used to seeing,' you see eyes open, and this whole new realm of possibilities presents itself,"[36] he said in a 2023 interview with Youth Today.

"Hobbies can be the one thing we do that doesn't even require us to be good at them."[37]

—Courtney Cope, mental health therapist

Making athletics and exercise a hobby also means not worrying about being the best or doing the activity with the hope that it will lead to school or career achievement. "Hobbies can be the one thing we do that doesn't even require us to be good at them," therapist Courtney Cope said in 2023 article in *Fortune*. "We can do them simply because we love them or because they make us feel good versus many of the other activities we do that make us money, help us stay productive, or that have a specific end goal in mind."[37]

Team Sports

If you've grown up playing soccer, basketball, or other team sports, then continuing to play as a teenager may come down to whether you have the skills and dedication to participate at a highly competitive level (high school varsity athletics or a club travel team) or your talents, schedule, and interests make a less-competitive recreational program a better fit. Finding time for team sports can be worth it because they promote good physical and mental health. A 2022 study in the *International Journal of Environmental Research and Public Health* suggests that young athletes who play sports tend to have lower levels of depression compared to their peers who don't play sports.

The camaraderie that develops through team sports can lead to close friendships now and lifelong friendships after you stop playing. National Basketball Association legend LeBron James was the only one of his high school and youth league teammates from Akron, Ohio, to play in the pros, but he remains close to them more than twenty years after they all graduated. "I speak to them almost every day," James told the *Akron Beacon Journal* in 2022. "We have that connection and that friendship that's been going on since we were 9 years old."[38]

If you'd like to start playing a team sport but have no experience, think about a recreational league, such as those sponsored by the YMCA or other youth sports program. To develop skills quickly, investigate summer sports camps or even instruction from online or local coaches.

Individual Sports

If you'd rather be alone in the competitive spotlight rather than be part of a team, think about individual sports, such as running, swimming, or gymnastics. While you can be part of a team in some of these sports, how you perform is primarily up to you alone. Many individual sports, including tennis and golf, can be enjoyed for many years.

Making Time for a Hobby

If you're already busy with school and extracurricular activities as well as responsibilities at home or at a part-time job, the idea of adding a time-consuming hobby may seem overwhelming. But if you step back and look at your schedule, you can probably find hidden blocks of time you can devote to a hobby. It might mean less time using your phone or playing video games, but the rewards of a new hobby will be worth it. A hobby doesn't have to be a daily activity. Maybe it's something you do just on the weekends or here and there throughout a given week or month. You may also realize that you have a lot of extra time that could be more productive or more interesting if you filled those hours with a new pastime. Taking little breaks, whether it's for a hobby or just a walk around the block, is also associated with being more productive. So instead of feeling guilty for working on a new yoga pose or a backside flip on your skateboard, remember that when you get back to your homework, you may be more focused and productive than you were just a few minutes before.

As with team sport participation, if you are new to an activity, have realistic expectations. You probably won't break any records the first time you run a mile or play a round of golf, but you might discover a sport that you will enjoy playing now and long into the future. When choosing a sport, do some research about the training involved and what it will take to improve your skills. Like most things, the better you get, the more fun an activity becomes. And to increase that level of enjoyment, try to recruit a friend to join you in your new athletic pursuit. After all, tennis is a lot more fun with someone you know on the other side of the net.

Martial Arts

People learn martial arts for a variety of reasons—to get in shape, learn self-defense, or find a competitive activity that simply feels like a good fit. Nikita Chaychenko, a junior at California's Roseville High School, started doing tae kwon do when he was four years old. He told his high school paper, the *Eye of the Tiger*, in 2022 that along the way to becoming a second-degree blackbelt and winning plenty of championships, martial arts improved his self-discipline and patience, as well as his fitness. "It is a good way to exercise, we do a lot of different things and use a lot of different muscles that you may not be used to," Chaychenko said. "In the beginning it's fun, but it gets harder as you progress as everything does, but if you stick with it I guarantee you will enjoy it."[39]

> **"In the beginning it's fun, but it gets harder as you progress as everything does, but if you stick with it I guarantee you will enjoy it."[39]**
>
> —Nikita Chaychenko, California high school student and tae kwon do champion

One of the advantages of martial arts as a hobby is that you can jump into the sport at just about any age and with no experience. Martial arts studios, whether they focus on tae kwon do, Brazilian jujitsu, karate, or any other martial art, usually offer classes for beginners on up through more experienced levels. Many studios even offer a lesson or two for free to let you decide whether that's the activity for you.

Martial arts improve participants' fitness, self-discipline, and patience, and unlike some sports, they can be practiced at any age.

Climbing and Hiking

Enjoying the great outdoors and getting a great workout at the same time is the win-win afforded by activities such as climbing and hiking. Local, state, and national parks usually have trails dedicated to hiking. And if you live in a hilly or mountainous region, parks departments may maintain areas for climbing, too. A little online research should help you find out where to explore.

Because of the nature of these activities, it's best to go with others in case of injury or emergency. Falls, animal encounters, or simply getting lost are risks that you can minimize by knowing the terrain and traveling with a group. Hiking and climbing clubs are great avenues for learning about everything from the right footwear and equipment to the best trails for beginners.

Of course, you don't always need actual rocks to do some rock climbing anymore. Many communities have indoor and outdoor climbing walls filled with artificial rocks, outcroppings, holes, and other features to simulate the challenges of an actual steep mountainside. And if you get particularly good at rock climbing (even the indoor variety), you can compete with others in state and national championships. Anchorage, Alaska, teenager Henrik Keskula competed in multiple national competitions but wasn't sure how much more he wanted to make of his hobby as he prepared to head off to college. "I'm definitely going to climb in college but I don't know if I'm necessarily going to climb competitively," Keskula told the *Anchorage Daily News* in 2023. "I'm leaving that open to whatever feels best for my life."[40]

Skateboarding

Sidewalks, driveways, empty swimming pools, and specially designed skate parks echo every day with the sound of rolling polyurethane wheels and the cheers (or painful howls) of kids trying tricks to impress their friends or meet their own personal challenges. Like so many simple outdoor activities, skateboarding saw a huge jump in popularity during the first couple of years

Thirteen-year-old Brazilian athlete Rayssa Leal competes at the Tokyo 2020 Olympic Games on July 26, 2021, taking the silver medal in women's street skateboarding.

of the COVID-19 pandemic. Statista research suggests that the number of people in the United States, including kids, who skateboarded regularly jumped from 6.6 million in 2019 to about 8.8 million in 2020. Skateboarding also drew new fans when it debuted in the Tokyo Olympics in 2021, and it quickly became a massive fan favorite.

While skateboarding can just be a way to get to your best friend's home, it can also be a hobby to enjoy on your own or with other skaters. To get started, consider going to a skateboard shop to find a board that's the right size for you and to get a well-fitting helmet and other safety gear. If you have a relative or friend who is into skateboarding, you may be able to borrow a board or at least get some good advice about how to get started. Skateboarding videos cover everything from the basics—how to stand on the board without falling off and how to push off the ground to keep going—to challenging tricks. Your local parks department may oversee a skate park or at least be able to direct you to safe and appropriate places to practice.

Yoga

While many physical activities can reduce stress while also getting you in better shape, there are few that accomplish both of those things as consistently as yoga. Through a slow-moving series of poses or postures, while also focusing on deep, steady breathing, a yoga practitioner can improve muscle strength and flexibility. Yoga classes also emphasize calm thinking that allows you to clear your mind while you're stretching your legs. And once you start taking yoga classes, you may find yourself striking those poses to help you manage stress away from the yoga studio. Indiana high school senior Julia Poertner began seeing a change in her coping practices not long after enrolling in her first yoga class. "I think mostly I've noticed that I've started trying to do movement techniques either if I'm frustrated or kind of feeling anxious,"[41] Poertner told the *Indianapolis Recorder* in 2023.

Yoga is another activity that you can start at any age with no experience at all. Classes are offered at yoga studios, as well as some fitness centers and schools. If you take a class and the instructor guides you to a pose that you're not ready for, you can always skip that one. You can also get started by watching videos, though don't try anything too physically strenuous without a trained instructor nearby. Yoga is a generally safe activity, but some poses, such as those involving headstands, can

Mental Health Benefits of Hobbies

In addition to having fun with a sport or activity, you can also improve your mental health with these hobbies, explains Matthew Zawadzki, an associate professor of health psychology at the University of California, Merced. He told the *Los Angeles Times* in 2023 that hobbies can divert your attention from things that might otherwise be stressing you out. "You're not ruminating and worrying about what's happening. You're invested in the moment, and so that restoration from the relaxation has big effects," he said. Research also shows that hobbies are associated with a greater sense of well-being, reduced levels of anxiety, and greater social connections. These benefits are associated with all kinds of hobbies, including sports, the arts, and other pursuits that you enjoy. But if you find that a hobby is triggering stress—perhaps you're burned out on a particular sport or activity—then take that as a sign that you should set that pastime aside for now and look for another outlet for your energy and attention.

Quoted in Emma Fox, "You Need a Hobby. Here's How to Find One That's Right for You," *Los Angeles Times*, August 30, 2023. www.latimes.com.

be very demanding. Take your time and work up to the more advanced levels of yoga. There's still plenty to be gained at the beginner level.

Other Physical Activity Hobbies

If your athletic interests lie outside the traditional youth sports, you may find your niche in other activities, such as fencing. Tulsa, Oklahoma, teen Sparrow Jaris gave fencing a try, at the urging of her father, to complement her other hobbies such as video games, robotics, and hiking. She joined the Tulsa Fencing Club and found her new sport exciting but very challenging. "I really like how nice the other fencers are," she told *TulsaKids* magazine. "Fencing is very rewarding but very difficult."[42]

Or maybe your new hobby will take you out on the water in a kayak, canoe, paddleboard, sailboat, or other watercraft. Look for rowing clubs in your area. Most offer programs for beginners all the way to options for more experienced rowers. Alabama-based

"I really love seeing the camaraderie between everyone that rows together, no matter what their skill level or experience."[43]

—Jackie Major, Alabama rowing coach

rowing coach Jackie Major says that while rowing can be a physically challenging sport, the teamwork required for a boat to move smoothly across the water is unlike any other activity. "I really love seeing the camaraderie between everyone that rows together, no matter what their skill level or experience. They appreciate one another and recognize how difficult the sport can be,"[43] he told the online news site Bham Now in 2020.

Some specialty hobbies can be expensive. The costs of riding horses, scuba diving, and even golf can add up. But supporting your hobby with a part-time job or looking for ways to cut costs by using preowned equipment or asking organizations about financial assistance may help keep these pursuits within reach.

SOURCE NOTES

Introduction: How Hobbies Help

1. Quoted in Paul Schattenberg, "The Positive Effects of Gardening on Mental Health," AgrilLife Today, April 25, 2022. https://agrilifetoday.tamu.edu.
2. Quoted in Tara Rittler, "From Fun to Future: Local Kids Discuss How Hobbies Shape Their Lives," *TulsaKids*, March 24, 2023. www.tulsakids.com.
3. Quoted in Emma Fox, "You Need a Hobby. Here's How to Find One That's Right for You," *Los Angeles Times*, August 30, 2023. www.latimes.com.
4. Quoted in Fox, "You Need a Hobby."
5. Quoted in Authority Magazine Editorial Staff, "Ten Entrepreneurs Share How They Turned Their Hobbies into Successful Careers," Medium, December 10, 2019. https://medium.com.

Chapter One: Hands-On Hobbies

6. Quoted in Robert Marchant, "Love of Tractors Turns 17-Year-Old Greenwich Student into a TikTok Star as Followers Watch Him Tinker," *Greenwich (CT) Time*, October 1, 2022. https://greenwichtime.com.
7. Quoted in Mark Wilson, "Bradenton Teen Finds Sweet Success by Turning Pandemic Hobby into Booming Business," FOX13 Tampa Bay, August 25, 2022. www.fox13news.com
8. Quoted in Julissa Garza, "Arkansas Teen's Hobby of Making Jewelry Leads to Non-profit," THV11, 2023. www.thv11.com.
9. Quoted in Luke Harold, "Local Students Reach Finals of National Rocketry Competition," *Del Mar (CA) Times*, April 17, 2023. www.delmartimes.net.
10. Quoted in Dustin George, "Teen Opens Community Garden in Lattimore," *Shelby (NC) Star*, May 19, 2021. www.shelbystar.com.
11. Monika Egerer et al., "Gardening Can Relieve Human Stress and Boost Nature Connection During the COVID-19 Pandemic," *Urban Forestry and Urban Greening*, February 2022. www.ncbi.nlm.nih.gov.
12. Quoted in Colette Victorino, "Santa Barbara Youth Zander Doherty Receives Woodworking National Recognition," *Santa Barbara (CA) Independent*, August 15, 2023. www.independent.com.

Chapter Two: Keep Your Brain Busy

13. Quoted in Marc Cota-Robles, "'Moon Girl Reads' TikTok Videos Encourage Others to Read, Expose Diverse Authors to Wider Audience," *ABC7 Eyewitness News*, September 29, 2022. www.abc7.com.
14. Quoted in Maya Dang, "Berkeley Poet Laureate Program Amplifies Youth Expression," *Berkeley High Jacket*, October 6, 2023. https://berkeleyhighjacket.com.
15. Quoted in Lynn Blinn Pike, "Journaling with Teens," University of Missouri Extension. https://extension.missouri.edu.
16. Quoted in University of Hawai'i News, "Teen Mentored by UH Astronomers Publishes Solar Research," March 1, 2022. www.hawaii.edu.
17. Quoted in Elizabeth Heubeck, "A Chess Grandmaster Makes the Case for Teaching the Game in School," *Education Week*, April 28, 2023. www.edweek.org.
18. Quoted in Ryan Clark, "Puzzling Behavior: CHS Student Travels to Spain for World Championships," University of Kentucky News, September 22, 2023. http://uknow.uky.edu.
19. Quoted in Benjamin Hart, "How an 18-Year-Old Got His Crossword Puzzle in the Sunday *Times*," *New York*, January 27, 2023. https://nymag.com.

Chapter Three: High-Tech Hobbies

20. Orhun Dalabasmaz, "A Brief History of Mine as a Computer Engineer," Medium, December 2, 2018. https://odalabasmaz.medium.
21. Quoted in Guy McCarthy, "Summerville High Students Learn to Write Code, Create Apps During 3-Week Course," *Sonora (CA) Union Democrat*, July 31, 2023. www.uniondemocrat.com.
22. Grant Darling, "Can Coding Be a Hobby? Why Coding Is a Good Hobby to Learn," *The Code Bytes* (blog), February 13, 2022. https://thecodebytes.com.
23. Quoted in Hunter Cloud, "The Hardest Fun: Technocats Are Going to Worlds," *Brookhaven (MS) Daily Leader*, March 9, 2023. www.dailyleader.com.
24. Quoted in Carlos Aguilar, "How a 14-Year-Old Came to Animate a Scene in 'Across the Spider-Verse,'" *New York Times*, June 7, 2023. www.nytimes.com.
25. Quoted in Emily St. Martin, "'Across the Spider-Verse' Added Another Remarkable Teen to the Movie—as an Animator," *Los Angeles Times*, June 14, 2023. wwww.latimes.com.
26. Quoted in Wayne State University School of Medicine News, "Warrior Spotlight: Class of 2025 M.D. Student Huda Warsame," July 11, 2023. https://today.wayne.edu.
27. Kenneth R. Rosen, "Curious About 3D Printing? Here Are Some Tips Before You Dive In," *Wired*, August 26, 2022. www.wired.com.

28. Quoted in Sal DiMaggio, "East Brunswick Teens Aim to Score Big with Sports Podcast," My Central Jersey, August 7, 2023. www.mycentraljersey.com.

Chapter Four: Hobbies and the Arts

29. Quoted in Robayet Hossain, "From Hobby to Career: Seniors Reflect on Their Musical Journeys," *Brown Daily Herald*, May 24, 2023. www.browndailyherald.com.
30. Quoted in Morgan Lahm, "5 Benefits of Playing a Musical Instrument in High School," *Teen Magazine*, July 14, 2022. www.theteenmagazine.com.
31. Quoted in Grace White, "This Houston-Area Girl Is Only 14 but She's Singing Her Way to Stardom," KHOU, July 3, 2023. www.khou.com.
32. Quoted in Rittler, "From Fun to Future."
33. Quoted in Alicia Adamczyk, "This 26-Year-Old Earns $78,000 per Year as a Full-Time Magician in New York City," CNBC Make It, February 17, 2022. www.cnbc.com.
34. Quoted in Jonathan Nelson, "Hobbies Help Distract from College Stress," *The All State*, October 19, 2020. www.theallstate.org.
35. Imogen Rosenberg, "Ceramics: The Go-to Hobby for Teens," *The Oarsmen*, October 12, 2023. https://veniceoarsmen.com.

Chapter Five: Time to Get Active

36. Quoted in Jacqueline Kantor, "'Yes, You Can Do This': The Story Behind the Rapid Rise in Sports for Youth with Disabilities," Youth Today, February 27, 2023. https://youthtoday.org.
37. Quoted in L'oreal Thompson Payton, "5 Reasons Why You Should Revisit Your Childhood Hobby as an Adult," *Fortune*, February 25, 2023. www.fortune.com.
38. Quoted in Marla Ridenour, "'Even More Special': LeBron James Reconnects with STVM Teammates During NBA All-Star Week," *Akron (OH) Beacon Journal*, February 19, 2022. www.beaconjournal.com.
39. Quoted in Rocky Moffitt, "Junior Brings Taekwondo to the Next Level," *Eye of the Tiger*, April 29, 2022. https://eyeofthetigernews.com.
40. Quoted in Josh Reed, "Anchorage Youth Rock Climbers Head to Nationals," *Anchorage (AK) Daily News*, July 8, 2023. www.adn.com.
41. Quoted in Chloe McGowan, "Wellness Programing in Schools Is Positively Impacting Students," *Indianapolis Recorder*, March 23, 2023. https://indiananapolisrecorder.com.
42. Quoted in Rittler, "From Fun to Future."
43. Quoted in Jon Eastwood, "Rowing on Lake Purdy—How You Can Learn to Row, Keep Fit and Meet New Friends," Bham Now, December 13, 2020. https://bhamnow.com.

FOR FURTHER RESEARCH

Books

Alex Carroll, *Yoga Poses for Beginners: YOGA!—50 Beginner Yoga Poses to Start Your Journey*. London: Readers First, 2023.

David Wayne Chiu, *Create Your Own Graphic Novel: A Guide for Kids*. New York: Rockridge, 2020.

Catherine V. Holmes, *How to Draw Cool Stuff: The 5 Minute Workbook*. New York: Library Tales, 2020.

Jessica Vitkus, *Crafting Change: Handmade Activism, Past and Present*. New York: Farrar, Straus and Giroux, 2022.

Peter Vogl, *Beginner Guitar Lessons Book 1*. East Point, GA: Watch & Learn, 2021.

Andrew Yeah, *JavaScript Coding for Teens: A Beginner's Guide to Developing Websites and Games*. New York: Rockridge, 2022.

Internet Sources

BostonTechMom, "Resource Guide to DIY STEM Projects for Teens," July 4, 2022. www.bostontechmom.com.

ClassPop!, "23 Fun and Easy Art Ideas Teens Will Love in 2023," June 14, 2023. www.classpop.com.

Nemours TeensHealth, "Choosing the Right Sport for You," 2023. https://kidshealth.org.

Raising Teens Today, "70 Cool Hobbies for Teens (That Aren't Boring)," 2023. https://raisingteenstoday.com.

U.S. News & World Report, "Find College Scholarships Related to Your Hobbies," February 27, 2023. www.usnews.com.

Utah State University, "How Hobbies Improve Mental Health," October 25, 2021. https://extension.usu.edu.

Websites

American Craft Council
www.craftcouncil.org
This organization sponsors crafting workshops as well as provides information and resources for people who want to turn their crafting into a business. The site includes instructional videos

from expert crafters and artists in which they offer tips and advice to those just starting out.

ASVAB Career Exploration Program
www.asvabprogram.com
This site explains how hobbies and extracurricular activities contribute to better mental health, career planning, and more well-rounded college applications. There are several helpful links, including an interest survey that can help you better understand the subjects and activities that inspire you.

Boys & Girls Clubs of America (BGCA)
www.bgca.org
This organization sponsors programs in sports, the arts, and other areas. Its website includes links to BGCA partners such as Play Ball, a youth baseball and softball program, and Lyricism 101, a program that encourages teens to express themselves through the music of hip hop culture. You can also find information about a wide range of summer and after-school programs.

National Aeronautics and Space Administration (NASA)
www.nasa.gov/learning-resources/for-students-grades-9-12
This section of NASA's site focuses on news, activities, and opportunities geared toward teens with an interest in space exploration and aerospace engineering. You can learn the latest about NASA programs and find ways to get involved with missions to the moon and Mars.

Read Across America
www.nea.org/professional-excellence/student-engagement/read-across-america
This National Education Association program features different themes every month, with recommended books and authors for all reading levels. You can explore book titles that deal with social justice, family stories, poetry, the environment, and many other topics. Read Across America also provides information about how to start a book club.

Stone Soup
https://stonesoup.com
This site includes information about how young writers (up to age thirteen) can get published, and it provides a list of many other outlets where teens and older students can publish their poetry, stories, and essays. You can also find links for online writing classes and workshops as well as a current calendar of writing contests.

INDEX

PICTURE CREDITS

Cover: Shutterstock.com

5: Pinkcandy/Shutterstock.com
9: VH-studio/Shutterstock.com
12: Gorodenkoff/Shutterstock.com
15: chomplearn/Shutterstock.com
18: sebra/Shutterstock.com
21: AstroStar/Shutterstock.com
23: TCD/Prod.DB/Alamy Stock Photo
28: ZUMA Press, Inc./Alamy Stock Photo
31: MarbellaStudio/Shutterstock.com
33: Stokkete/Shutterstock.com
37: Monkey Business Images/Shutterstock.com
39: Sipa USA/Alamy Stock Photo
42: Prathankarnpap/Shutterstock.com
46: PeopleImages.com - Yuri A/Shutterstock.com
49: Roman Kosolapov/Shutterstock.com
51: A.RICARDO/Shutterstock.com

ABOUT THE AUTHOR

After graduating from the University of Oregon, James Roland became a newspaper reporter, primarily focused on education. He later became a magazine writer and editor, as well as the author of more than a dozen books. He and his wife, Heidi, have three children, Chris, Alexa, and Carson.